*D*ear Parent,

The Anne of Green Gables Seri
to raise social and educational issues that will benefit young children.

Anne is a strong female character with a colorful vocabulary and a vibrant imagination. Her vocabulary level is meant to stimulate the reading experience for young people. Inserted on the final pages of this book is a handy dictionary for clarification of certain words and expressions.

Step into Anne's world and benefit from her desire to build friendships and inspire others through her wonderful imagination and her determination to succeed!

Log on to **www.learnwithanne.com** and explore an educational guide, with outlines of lesson plans and discussion topics available for teachers and parents alike.

Also check out **www.annetoon.com** for educational games, activities and multimedia that bring Anne's character and friends to life.

Published in 2010 by Davenport Press
110 Davenport Rd.
Toronto, Ontario, M5R 3R3

Printed in Canada

ISBN = 978-0-9736803-3-1

anne of green gables

AS SEEN ON
PBS

Anne's RED HAIR

KEVIN **SULLIVAN** &
LESLIE **GOLDMAN**

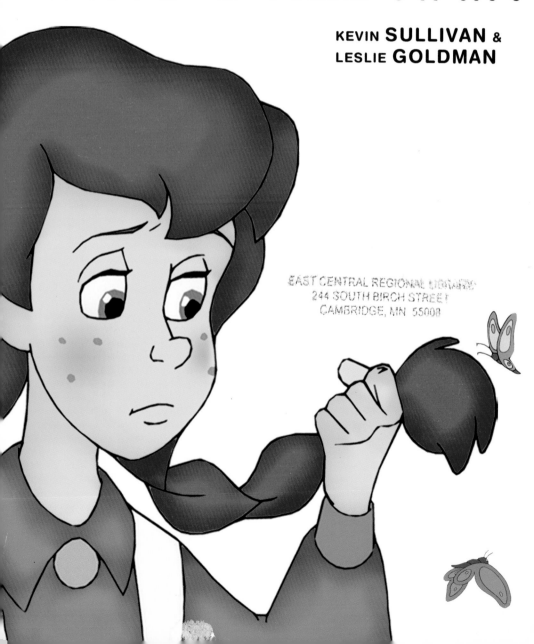

Anne was very
sensitive about the
color of her hair.

She complained
to her adoptive
mother, Marilla.

"I am tired of
my red hair!"

Anne watched Marilla
use lemon juice to wash
out a red strawberry stain.
That gave her an idea.

Anne squeezed lemon juice into her hair. Diana helped her.

"People like you for who you are, not for what color your hair is."

Anne looked at her reflection and frowned. Her hair was still bright red!

But Anne would not give up. She made a blond wig out of a mop!

Diana and Anne walked to town. Anne wore her new hair.

Gilbert ran by and pulled off Anne's wig!

Anne and Diana met a man selling hair dye on the road.

"This will make your hair a beautiful raven black."

Anne bought the hair dye.

11

Diana washed the tonic into Anne's hair
When Diana finished, Anne looked
in a mirror.

12

**After Diana left, Anne began to cry.
She started to daydream.**

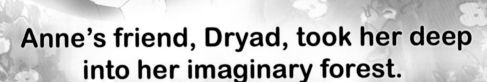

"If only I wasn't different. If only I was pretty!"

**Anne's friend, Dryad, took her deep
into her imaginary forest.**

They heard beautiful music.

"Look, there's the Fairy Trio!"

They saw a fairy playing a harp.
The harp was made from
her green hair!

Beside her came
a gentle sound
from the Gap
Goblin,

while a Nose Gnome sat
playing his large fat
nose.

15

Anne left her imaginary friends and quickly ran home.

Marilla washed her
hair with vinegar.
It became fiery red,
once again.

The next day Gilbert admitted that he really liked Anne.

Especially because she always had a quick answer everytime he teased her.

Later on, Anne found Dryad again. She whispered to him that having "kindred spirits" like Matthew, Marilla, Diana and even Gilbert meant so much more to her than the color of her hair.

Dryad promised to return
whenever Anne needed to
solve a problem.

Anne's Fancy Dancy Words

Avonlea - the town where Anne lives

Concept - idea

Dye - hair color

Gnome - elf with long nose

Goblin - imaginary creature

Anne's Fancy Dancy Words

Harmonious - things that work togethe

Kindred spirits - best friends

Reflection - a mirror image

Tonic - potion